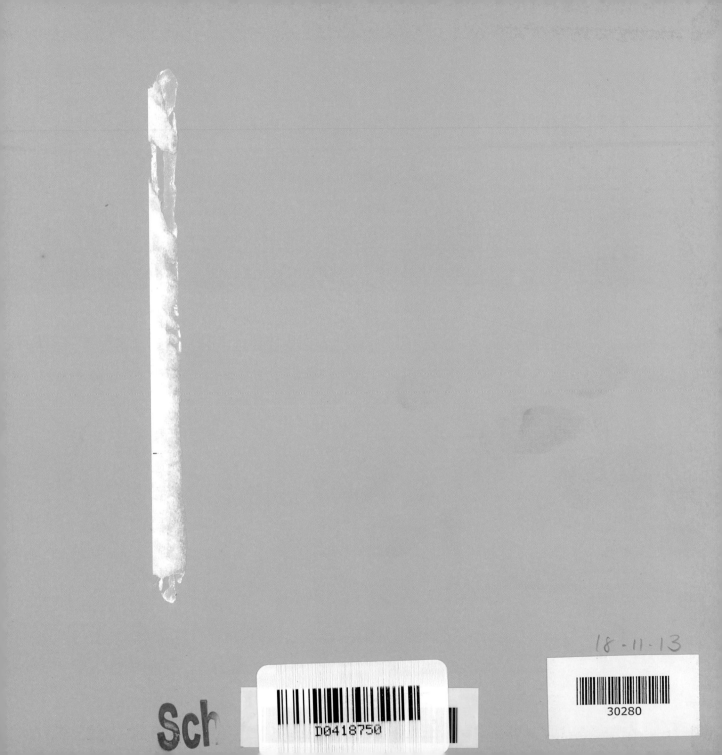

For Wilf

WHERE WE LIVE
A HUTCHINSON BOOK 0 09 188497 7

Published in Great Britain by Hutchinson,
an imprint of Random House Children's Books

This edition published 2004

1 3 5 7 9 10 8 6 4 2

RANDOM HOUSE CHILDREN'S BOOKS
61–63 Uxbridge Road, London W5 5SA
A division of The Random House Group Ltd

RANDOM HOUSE AUSTRALIA (PTY) LTD
20 Alfred Street, Milsons Point, Sydney,
New South Wales 2061, Australia

RANDOM HOUSE NEW ZEALAND LTD
18 Poland Road, Glenfield, Auckland 10, New Zealand

RANDOM HOUSE (PTY) LTD
Endulini, 5A Jubilee Road, Parktown 2193, South Africa

THE RANDOM HOUSE GROUP Limited Reg. No. 954009
www.kidsatrandomhouse.co.uk

A CIP catalogue record for this book is available from the British Library.

Printed in Singapore

Where We Live

Reg Cartwright

HUTCHINSON
LONDON SYDNEY AUCKLAND JOHANNESBURG

I am a tiger and I live in the jungle.

I am a whale and I live in the sea.

I am a crocodile and I live in the river.

I am a bird and I live in a tree.

I am a duck and I live on a pond.

I am a goldfish
and I live in a bowl.

I am a grub and I live in an apple

and I live underground
because I'm a mole.

I am a fox and I live in the woods.

We are sheep and we live on a farm.

We sleep all day and come out at night.

We are owls and we live in a barn.

I am a polar bear and I live in the snow.

I am a lizard,
I live under a stone.

I am a zebra and I live on the plain.

I am a tortoise,
my shell is my home.

I am a spider and I live in a web.

We are elephants
and we live in a herd.

We are bees and we live in a hive.

I live on a leaf. I'm a ladybird!

I am a rabbit and I live in a burrow.

I can live anywhere
because I'm a mouse.

I am a camel and I live in the desert

and we are children and
we live in a house.